Hello, Reader!

Minnie is too busy to play.
She is eating spaghetti!
Can Freddy stop her?

Find out in this
funny book.

Library of Congress Cataloging-in-Publication Data
Gelman, Rita Golden.
    More spaghetti, I say / by Rita Golden Gelman ; illustrated by
Mort Gerberg.
        p.   cm.—(Hello reader)
    "Level 1."
    Summary: Minnie the monkey is too busy eating spaghetti—all day,
in all ways—to play with Freddy.
    ISBN 0-590-90749-2
    [1. Stories in rhyme. 2. Monkeys—Fiction. 3. Spaghetti—
Fiction. 4. Humorous stories.] I. Gerberg, Mort. ill.
II. Title. III. Series.
PZ8.3.G28MO   1992
[E]—dc20   91-43181
                                                                CIP
                                                                AC

6 5   9/9
                                                             24
Printed in the U.S.A.
First Scholastic Printing, January 1993

More Spaghetti, I Say!

by Rita Golden Gelman
Illustrated by Mort Gerberg

Hello Reader! — Level 2

SCHOLASTIC INC.

New York　　Toronto　　London　　Auckland　　Sydney

"Play with me, Minnie.
Play with me, please.

We can stand on our heads.
We can hang by our knees."

"Oh, no.
I can't play.
I can't play with you, Freddy.

Not now.
Can't you see?
I am eating spaghetti."

"Now you can do it.
Now you can play.

We can jump on the bed
for the rest of the day."

"No. I can **not**.
I can **not** jump and play.
Can't you see?
I need more.

More spaghetti, I say!

I love it.
I love it.
I love it.
I do.

I love it so much!"

"More than me?"

"More than you.

I love it on pancakes
with ice cream and ham.
With pickles and cookies,
bananas and jam.

I love it with mustard
and marshmallow stuff.
I eat it all day.
I just can't get enough.

I eat it on trucks,
and I eat it in trees."

"You eat it too much.
Won't you play with me,
PLEASE?"

"I can run in spaghetti.

And ride in spaghetti.

I can jump.
I can slide.
I can hide
in spaghetti.

I can skate on spaghetti,
and ski on spaghetti.

And look at this picture.
That's me on spaghetti."

"Spaghetti. Spaghetti. That's all you can say. I am going to throw your spaghetti away.

I am going to throw it
all over the bed,
in the air,
on your chair,
on the floor,
ON YOUR HEAD!

Oh, Minnie,
that look on your face!
You look bad.
You look big.
You look green.
You look sick.
You look sad."

"You are right.
I am green.
I feel sick.
Yes, I do.
I think I will rest.
I will sit here with you."

"Let me take this away now.
I think that I should.

And then we can play.

Mmmmmmmm!
Spaghetti is good.

I love it.
I love it.
I love it.
I do.
I need more spaghetti.
I can't play with you."

"But **now** I can play.
I can play with you, Freddy."

"Not now.
Can't you see?

I am eating spaghetti."